Spike and Mike

BY NANCY HALL AND MARY PACKARD
ILLUSTRATED BY LISA McCUE

CHILDRENS PRESS ®

CHICAGO

Printed in the United States of America. Published by Grolier Direct Marketing, Danbury, Connecticut.
Design by Antler & Baldwin Group. ISBN 0-516-00830-7

A SPIKE & MIKE™ BOOK   PRINTED ON RECYCLED PAPER

When the big storm came to Mangrove Marsh, things
got all mixed up.

It blew the roof clear off Rapid Rabbit's house.

Mr. Swamp Fox got stuck in Miss Bobcat's chimney.

And when Mrs. Gator checked her nursery, she worried that one of her eggs might be missing.

The wind and the rain swept through Mrs. Egret's
nursery, too.

"Are all of my eggs still here?" she wondered.

Finally the rain stopped. The howling wind became a gentle breeze, and life returned to normal in Mangrove Marsh.

Normal, that is, except for a couple of eggs that were still floating down the river.

The two little eggs raced right past Old Man Otter's general store.

They floated by Turtle Island and traveled all the way down the canal. At last they came to rest at the edge of a lily pond in Cypress Glade.

The two eggs had barely settled down in the soft sweet grass on the bank of the pond when one of them began to quiver and shake. The animal inside began to peck and chip. At last there was a great big **CRACK!**

"Whew," said a baby alligator as he climbed out of his shell. "It sure was getting cramped in there!"

Just then he noticed the other egg nestled beside him.

"I have a brother or sister!" the alligator exclaimed happily, and he sat down beside the egg to wait...and wait...and wait.

When it was nightfall, the world became dark and lonely. The alligator looked at the egg. "I won't be lonely for long," he said to himself. Then he whispered, "Won't you please hurry up?"

The alligator waited two days and two nights before the second egg began to quiver and shake.

"Finally," the alligator cried. And it wasn't long before he heard some pecking and chipping and a great big **CRACK!** The alligator watched as a tiny head poked out of its shell.

"Mama!" cried a newborn baby bird.

"I'm not your mama!" laughed the alligator. "I'm your brother."

The little alligator and the little bird looked at each other carefully.

"We sure look different," said the bird.

"I like your soft feathers," said the alligator.

"And I like your spiky back."

"*Spike*," repeated the bird. "That's what I'll call you."

"Then I'll call you *Mike*," said the alligator. "We may not look the same, but at least our names sound alike!"

"Where is our nest?" asked Mike.

"*Nest?*" repeated Spike, squishing his toes in the mud. "I thought we would live on the ground by the edge of the pond."

"In the *mud?*" asked Mike, with surprise. "A home should be dry, not damp," he explained, fluffing his pretty white feathers.

Suddenly out of nowhere, voices chimed in.
"The best homes are underground," offered a timid
young bunny.

"Sticks," said a roly-poly beaver. "You can't beat a house made of sticks. I could help you build it."

"Lily pads," croaked Gumbo the frog. "My brother and I find lily pads make quite a nice home."

"Quite nice," croaked his brother, Jumbo, in agreement.

Soon Spike and Mike were surrounded by animal friends, each with a different idea about what type of home they should build.

"Ridiculous!" hissed Slink, slithering up to the group. "You two can't make a home together anyway. Mike is a bird. Birds live in trees. Spike is an alligator. Alligators live down low near the water."

"But we're brothers," explained Mike.

"Brothers?" all the animals said at once. "How can a bird and an alligator be brothers?"

"I don't know," answered Spike, "but we are. We're brothers because we hatched right here side by side."

The beaver scratched her head. The frog brothers shrugged their shoulders. Soon everyone began talking at once.

"What's all this racket about?" asked Tallulah, the big old swamp turtle, peeping her head out of her shell. "If they say they're brothers, then they are."

The other animals hesitated. None of them ever questioned Tallulah, the oldest and wisest of them all.

"But they don't even look the same," said Scarlett, a pretty flamingo, in a very small voice.

"Brothers don't have to look alike," Tallulah explained. "And they don't have to act the same either. If these two guys hatched right here side by side, then they must be brothers."

"Do you know what kind of home we should make?"
Mike asked. But by then, Tallulah had closed her eyes
and pulled her head back into her shell.

Spike looked at the cool wet earth in the shade of the twisted old cypress tree where Tallulah slept. Mike looked at the big branches high above the ground. Then Spike looked up high at the branches and Mike looked down low at the earth.

At that moment they knew exactly what they had to do. They would build a home like no other home in Cypress Glade—one that would be just right for both of them.

"We'll have two floors," said Spike. "I'll live downstairs..."

"And I'll live upstairs," cried Mike, flapping his wings in excitement.

Some of their friends helped Mike build the top floor high up in the tree.

The others worked down below with Spike. All the animals worked and worked until at last Spike and Mike had the perfect home.

And that is how a baby alligator named Spike and a little white bird named Mike came to be brothers and live together in a big old cypress tree in Cypress Glade.